Dedication

Thank you to my inspiration and heartbreaker. Just another man expressing love without knowing what the word really meant, you showed me what real connection looked like and what real heartbreak felt like. Thank you for inspiring my writing. You may never truly know the affect you had on me.

Table of Contents

I. Hush

Don't say a word.
Don't even think it.
It's too good to be true.
Don't you dare believe it.

You know how this goes.
You've been here before.
It'll always end the same,
Won't it?

Same game.
Different pieces.
Don't say a word.
Don't speak it.

Don't think it.

It's too good to be true.

Hush.

Don't ruin it.

II. Random Thoughts

Jumping through ropes hoping you'll admit

That we could be great, yet

Here we are,

Minding our own business,

Even though we know our

Lives could be greater

That we go great together

Like peanut butter and jelly

Yes, deliciously amazing

You and I

We are

Existing

Perfection

Sometimes.

III. Scattered Thoughts of You

Dark and lovely -- my nickname for you
Skin so smooth, eyes so true
You smile at me, my whole world begins anew

My feelings for you are like no other
Breathtakingly beautiful
Your mind takes me over
I've never felt like this before
Breathe me in as I breathe you in
Never keeping score
We live inside each other
Haunted forever

I don't know if this will be a great piece or
If this will be an absolute tragedy
I hope that you understand that
We could be a masterpiece
If you just let me give you a piece
Of my heart
Of my soul
Of love
Oh, my love
Because that's what I want
For us to become one
Through and through
As we live together
In harmony forever
Yes an eternity
You and I together

So

Thank you for giving me a reason
To really believe in
Those three faithful words:
I love you
I love you
Forever
I truly do

IV. Honesty

Honestly, honesty escapes me

When I look at you and consider what we could be

Honestly, I'm scared of the uncertainty

Honestly, I'm afraid of what might be

What this may mean

Maybe

Possibly

What could be

You and me

Honestly, honesty is a difficult thing

To manage, accept, declare, discuss

Describe, desire, attain, inquire

Honesty

Honestly, honesty escapes me

When I look back at this poem

What am I really saying?

Honestly,

In all honesty,

Honesty escapes me

I hope you don't

Honestly, that's in all honesty

Truthfully,

I want to see what this could be

And now I'm rambling

Honestly,

Honesty escapes me.

V. Love's Epitaph

Love died with weighted lies.
Drowning screams of goodbye
Suffocate life as I cry
Out for salvation.
Silence whispers:
Why?

VI. Afterthoughts on the Aftermath

Same game, different pieces.
A lie is a lie, a heartbreak is a heartbreak.
Let's not pretend this is anything different.
Call a spade a spade.
This is how it would always end.

No. Not the end.
I refuse to believe it.
I'll give you time.
Eventually you'll see it.

I am not naive.
I am not desperate.
I just have hope.
Eventually you'll see it.

This is just the beginning.
You might have trouble believing it.
You might not trust yourself
Or think you deserve it.

But I know your heart.
I meant it when I said it.
Being deserving of love doesn't mean you're perfect.
It just means you keep trying.
It just means you're worth it.

You're worth the effort.
You're worth taking a chance on.

You're worth risking it all for.
You're worthy of love.
I'll send this to you eventually.
I just need time or something more.

I need to process what just happened.
I need to stop crying.
I need to breathe again.
I need to stop hurting.
I need to hold on to hope.

Because I still believe it.
You are worth the risk.
You are worthy of love.
You are worth it all.
You just need to accept it.

VII.Closing Time

Closing up shop

It just hurts too much

Won't catch me again

My heart plays too much

Tears run through my veins

My eyes bleed too much

Pain beats through my chest

My heart hurts too much

I'm done

I'm closing up shop

This pain is just too much

Look what you made me do

I just cry too much

VIII. True Confessions

It was crazy to get so attached so quickly

I barely knew you but felt you were my destiny

Silly me

Foolish girl

I now see more clearly

It was never meant to be

I can never truly be happy

Alone in this world, watching people live

To die in this world, never really to live

I thought you were my meant to be

My destiny

My happy ending

Silly me

Stupid me

It was never meant to be

I can never just be happy

IX. Love's Etch

What do you do when your love begins to fade and all you have left is a dirty imprint of something that used to be so beautiful-- something you once thought would be eternal? A stained pain etched on your body is all that remains. Do you continue to try to clean it or do you simply watch until it disappears completely-- never to be seen again?

                                                     I think I'll choose the latter.

X. Questions Unanswered

Life. What is it other than a series of painful memories and broken promises scattered across a desolate future, void of any light?

Life. A conundrum wrapped in a paradox of oversimplified lies and intricate lines of disappointment from truths.

Life. What is life but a sad song on repeat, beautifully somber but killing joy not so softly.

Life. What's the point?

To live, to die -- rebirth to another death. We're here and then we're not.

Dust. Life. Why?

What's the point?

XI. Sad, But True

I loved you,
I love you,
I don't know which.
You broke my heart,
Stomped my heart,
Yes, you shattered it.
Fire engulfed my every emotion.
Tears drown my very existence.
Crying, screaming, hurting, longing.
Aching, bleeding, empty, buried
Alive or dead I don't know which.
I loved you,
I love you,
I don't ... yes I do.
It's sad,
Pathetic,
But it's true --
I love you.
I love you.
Forever, I still do.

XII. Mental Anguish

Slowly but surely

My anxiety is growing

Rising not falling

It seeks to engulf me

Chest tightening

Heavy breathing

There's no way to console me

Breaths quickening

Mind racing

I keep trying to keep steady

I try to hold on

But I lose my footing

I try not to fall

But I just keep on sinking

Further and further down

Into the dark abyss of depression

Spiraling, free falling

There's no fighting gravity

You did this to me

You made me worse

You took my hope

You broke my heart

Spiraling, free falling

Out of control

I tried to hold on so tight

Now I'll try letting go

Of you

Of us

It's time to say goodbye

Farewell

So long

I can't promise I won't cry

Chest tightening

Heart pounding

Eyes crying

Mouth screaming

Silently

I try

I fight

I can't

I tried

I fought

I cried

I can't

Stop

Don't do this

Don't leave me

You're gone

Stop

Don't do this

I can't lose you

You're gone

Spiraling farther

Into psychosis

Crying

Drowning

No remedy to get

Through this

Anxiety

Depression

My two closest friends

They never leave me

Not really

Maybe only for a moment

But you opened the door wide

Welcomed them back

Hello old friends

Come on in

Hope just left

Goodbye

XIII. Four, 3, Two, 1

I have no anger towards you
No bitterness
No malice
I only have sadness

I can't remember what life was like
Before you entered it
Before you invaded

I hate that I don't hate you
All I have left is love

I can't keep this up

I have to be done

XIV. Words From Beyond

Death becomes me

Sweet sorrow welcomes me

Like a warm blanket on a winter night

It shelters me

Comforts me

It is my home

I welcome it

As it welcomes me

We become one

Husband and wife

One flesh

Deteriorating together

Eternally stricken

With pain

With grief

With heartache

Until that one faithful night

When all goes silent

And all that is left

Is me

Death

We are one

Until the end of time

We just

Are
One

XV. The Whole Truth and Nothing But

I miss you.

That's right,

I have decided to write the truth.

No hidden meanings,

No skirting around the issue,

No attempts to protect my heart or reputation --

I miss you.

I miss you more than I thought it possible to miss someone.

I dream of you.

I dream of our past, have nightmares of our present, and fantasize of our future.

I miss you.

I miss your laugh, your smile, your brain, your kindness, your heart, your height, your awkwardness, your admiration, your voice... God, do I miss your voice!

That deep baritone that could lull me into a calm and push all my anxieties and fears away.

You made me feel... SAFE.

Like a deep exhale of relief,

You were that for me -- relief.

I thought I was safe with you.

I thought that would never change.

I miss you.

I'm afraid of how much I do.

I miss you with every fiber of my being.

I miss you when I'm awake and when I am asleep.

I miss you every day, hour, minute, and second.

I'm afraid that although I miss you so dearly,

You may not miss me.

I'm afraid that even if you do miss me, we'll never find our way back to each other.

I miss you.

I miss you more than any words could describe.

I miss you more than the sun misses the moon.

More than the sky misses the earth,

but our distance seems just as great if not more...

I miss you.

I thought you were it.

I thought I was done missing someone that didn't miss me.

I thought you were my meant to be.

I still do.

I guess that's why I can't let it go.

It's why in all honesty,

If I'm telling the truth and nothing but,

No matter what I do,

I will never not miss you.

I miss you.

That's my truth.

XVI. Crimes of the Heart

Villain.

The only kind I attract.

Thieves of the heart

Murderers of hope

Kidnapers of feelings

Villains.

Why does this keep happening?

Is it me?

Villain.

Maybe I'm the true villain

Destroying my destiny

Perpetually

Villain.

Liar to all

Honest to none

Villain.

Slain,

Beaten,

Gone.

There is only one

True

Villain.

XVII. Closure

Closure
What does it mean?
Is this an ending
Or is this a beginning
To begin anew
Without thoughts of you
Haunting me
Eternally
Memories of you.
Closure.
Is this the final curtain call?
Or is this just the end of
Act I.

XVIII. Relapse

Every time I think I'm through
I always come running back to you
Tug of war that I can't win
Emotional blackmail, I always give in
To you, it's been over for quite a while
Clear as day but all the meanwhile
I can't breathe without you
Knowing it's over and we're through
All I want is you back
But I'll settle for this constant relapse
Swimming deep in my emotions
Drowning in love's turbulent oceans
I thought I was done
But I guess that was just Act 1.

XIX. Hello

My heart cries out
For you
For love
For lust
For truth
For comfort
For love

Love...

But all it hears is nothing
Silence

Silence answers chillingly
Reminding me
Of your absence
Of your apathy
Of my loneliness
Of my sadness

Sadness

Calling constantly
There is no answer
No one is home
I'm empty
Hello?
Can you hear me?

I miss you
My heart is crying out
I miss you

Do you?

XX. Late Night Confessions

Love makes you crazy. It's complicated and hard. It burns a hole through your heart, through your soul. When it ends, the residue doesn't. You never forget. Your body never forgets. I can't forget. I feel claustrophobic. My chest is tight. I can't breathe without you. My heart struggles to learn how to beat again without you. You don't care. Maybe you never really did. I was so foolish. How could I believe that I could be happy? How could I believe in you? I trusted you. Fool. But then again, love makes you crazy. People always leave. I loved you. Love made me crazy. Love has left me crazy. Love left me. You left me. Nothing left but a hole that you burned right through me. My love has left me and I have no more love to give. Not again. You left me crazy and empty. Totally empty. You left me. I can't breathe without you. Love makes you crazy. Love is a difficult thing: to define, to describe, to find, to keep, to forget, to hide. Love makes you crazy. Love makes you lose your mind.

XXI. Goodbye

Goodbye my love.
You came and went
You stole my heart and ran.

Goodbye my love
You left your pain
You left me crying, ashamed.

Goodbye my love.
You broke my heart
You let the pieces burn.

Goodbye to you
My always boo
We'll never meet again.

XXII. To You

Today I cried 1 million tears and drowned 1 death for you.
A death so deep, my lips so blue, all in the name of you.
Today laid my head to rest and stretched my arms up high.
I cried and cried, I tried but died, all in the name of you.
Today I said my last goodbye, my last goodbye to you.
I'll stretch and fly, soaring up high, waving so long to you.

CPSIA information can be obtained
at www.ICGtesting.com
Printed in the USA
BVHW040250101218
535216BV00022B/958/P

9 781730 886799